Lesley York
Illustrations by Rosalyn Fenton

Emily's Shopping Surprise

Bumblebee Books
London

BUMBLEBEE PAPERBACK EDITION

Illustrations by Rosalyn Fenton

A CIP catalogue record for this title is
available from the British Library.

ISBN: 978-1-83934-325-4

Bumblebee Books is an imprint of
Olympia Publishers.

First Published in 2021

Bumblebee Books
Tallis House
2 Tallis Street
London
EC4Y 0AB

Printed in Great Britain

www.olympiapublishers.com

Acknowledgements

I would like to thank Rosalyn Fenton who has done all of the illustrations for me and my husband for helping with some of the editing. Also a big thank you to Olympia for publishing my book.

Chapter 1

Emily and her family all live in Winchester. One day she was going into town with her mummy and daddy. She was having a lovely time walking past all the shop's looking in the windows at the lovely clothes and pointing out lots of nice things, but when they walked passed one of the shop doorways Emily noticed a little bundle of fur in the corner of the doorway. It was shivering and shaking. "Mummy, Mummy what do you think that is?"

Her mummy and daddy said, "We don't know."

Mummy said, "Don't touch it, you don't know what it is."

"But, Mummy, it looks frightened."

Emily begged and begged to go over, to see what it was. In the end Emily's mummy and daddy said, "OK, let's go and have a look."

When they all got closer to the doorway Emily said, "It looks like a puppy, oh it looks so frightened, can we keep it please, please let's take it home."

Emily's mummy and daddy had puzzled looks on their faces, in the end they both said, "OK, just for one night, but we must find out if the puppy belongs to anyone first." So when they got home Emily gave the puppy some water and food.

The next day Emily's parents said, "We must contact the RSPCA first just to check to see if the puppy belongs to anyone before we take it to the vets."

The RSPCA called them back to give them good news, the puppy did not belong to anyone and if they wanted to keep it, they must take it to the vets to get it checked over. Emily was jumping up and down on the spot with joy.

They all jumped in the car and went off to the vets.

The vet checked the puppy over and said it looks very well it just needs lots of love and food. Emily was so excited she said, "Can we keep the puppy?"

"Yes you can but first it has to be microchipped."

The vet also said it's a little girl puppy. Emily had a big a smile on her face. "Here you are, dear," the vet said. "This is your new puppy."

"Mummy, Mummy what are we going to call her?"

"I don't know, my darling, why don't you think of a name as she is going to be your puppy."

"Alright, mummy, I will have a think."

In the car on their way home, Emily was thinking very hard, (think, think, now what can I call her!)

She thought of all sorts of names then all of a sudden, she shouted out in the car and made every one jump.

"I have it, I have it!"

"Have what?" said Mummy.

"A name for the puppy. I will call her Skye."

"Skye?" said Daddy, "Why?"

"Well it is a lovely sunny day and there is a lovely blue sky and I am so happy."

Emily's parents chuckled, it is a lovely name.

Chapter 2

The next day, Emily and her mummy went to the pet shop to get Skye her new bed.

"Mummy, can I have a pink collar for her and a lead please?"

"Yes OK."

"Shall we get her some toys to play with, Mummy?"

Emily could not wait to get home to show Skye all of her new things. When they both arrived home, Emily put the lovely pink collar on Skye. "You look so pretty," she said.

She then showed her, her new bed. They were both so excited. Emily was laughing, running around and rolling on the floor they were having so much fun.

Emily's mummy went to call her in as it was tea time. She found them both curled up together in Skye's bed fast asleep.

Her mummy calls out to her husband to come and see.

"See what?" he said. "Oh don't they both look lovely. She has really taken to the puppy."

"Yes she has, and Skye is going to be a good companion for her."

It was Monday morning. Emily's mummy called, "Come on you are going to be late for school."

"Aww but, but."

"No buts, you have to go to school."

"Can I take Skye with me?"

"No, Skye has to stay at home with me."

"But, Mum."

"No."

“Oh, all right.” Emily walks off with a long face. She went over to Skye to say goodbye and gave her a big kiss. “I have to go to school now but I will be back later.” Skye looked up at her with a smiley face.

Chapter 3

When Emily got to school she could not wait to let everyone know she had got a puppy.

When they were all in the classroom, the teacher said, “Can you all draw a picture of what you did at the weekend.”

Emily started drawing her mummy, daddy and herself, walking though Winchester and finding the puppy in the shop doorway. The teacher saw what she was drawing and asked her what it was about. “This is my new puppy, Miss Jones. We found her at the weekend.”

“She looks lovely. What have you called her?”

“Her name is Skye.”

“Oh that’s a pretty name.”

“Yes,” said Emily.

Her teacher said, “Shall we tell everyone in class?”

Emily looked puzzled, then said, “Yes, I would like that.”

Then Miss Jones went to the front of the class and said, “Quiet everyone, Emily has something lovely to say.”

Emily stood up in front of the class and showed the picture of the puppy. They all shouted, "You got a puppy," with excitement.

They were all talking at the same time, Emily could not hear what they were saying. Miss Jones said, "Calm down, only one at a time. Give Emily a chance to speak."

Emily said, "She is a lovely puppy. We found her in Winchester when I was shopping with my mummy and daddy." "Where did you find her?" they all called.

"She was in a shop doorway. Oh she is so lovely."

One of the children called, "What have you called her?"

"Skye," said Emily.

All of the children said, "You are so lucky."

"But first we had to check with the RSPCA to make sure she did not belong to anyone."

Emily was playing in the play ground with her best friend Dottie. She was asking lots of question about the puppy.

Emily said, "Ask your mummy if you can come round for tea then you can see Skye."

Dottie said, "Skye? Who's Skye?"

"That's the name of my puppy."

"Oh, that's a pretty name."

The next day after school Dottie came round for tea. Emily showed her the puppy and they went out in the garden to play together.

All three of them were having great fun rolling in the grass and throwing the ball for Skye to catch. There was so much laughter, it was lovely for the parents to watch. Emily's mummy called, "Come on in now it is time to eat."

"Oh, Mum, we are having so much fun."

"Yes come on now and Skye wants her tea as well.

"OK then."

And they all came in with big smiles on their faces.

Chapter 4

The following morning Emily woke up with a big stretch and rubbing her eyes. She started looking for Skye. She was fast asleep at the bottom of her bed. All of a sudden Skye woke up and was jumping all over her. Emily said, “Alright, alright I will let you out.” So down the stairs they run making a lot of noise, waking up her mummy and daddy. They said, “What is all that noise? Oh it’s only Emily and Skye,” they laughed.

Emily said, “Come Skye, lets go out in the garden to play.”

When they were out there playing Emily had

an idea. “I know what you can do,” she said to herself. She put obstacles all round the garden for Skye to jump over. At first it was funny as Skye just sat and watched Emily running round all of them. Skye had a big smile on her face. Emily kept calling her to follow her but she just sat there.

Emily called, “Mum, Mummy!” she shouted.

Emily’s mummy replied, “What do you want?”

“How do I get Skye to do this?”

“Do what?” her mummy asked.

“I want her to jump over all of these things I have put down.”

"Well what about if you use some of her food as a treat?"

"Ah, that's a good idea, I will try that."

Emily's parents looked out of the window to see her and Skye running and jumping over all of the things she had put down, they both had big grins on their faces.

The next day her parents were talking about what they saw Emily doing in the garden the day before. They wondered if it would be a good idea if Emily and Skye did some sort of training. So Emily's daddy said, "I will have to do some investigating to see what training classes are around."

When Emily was at school the next day she told Dottie what she was doing with Skye in the garden. Dottie said, "That sounds like good fun. I wish I could have a puppy then we could do things together."

“Yes that would be great,” said Emily. “Why don’t you ask your mummy if you could have a puppy too?”

“I will ask Mummy tonight,” said Dottie.

Chapter 5

Emily's daddy came home from work with some exciting news. While they were sitting at the dinner table her daddy said to Emily that he had found somewhere they could go and have lots of fun together. "Can Skye come too, Daddy?"

"Oh," he laughed, "yes of cause. It's for you and Skye."

Emily was so excited. "What have you found for us to do, Daddy?"

"Well how would you and Skye like to go to agility classes?"

"What's agility classes?" she asked with a puzzled look on her face. So her daddy explained.

"That sounds really great fun. When can we go?"

When Emily went to school the next day, she was talking to Dottie about the agility classes. "Oh, you are so lucky it sounds good fun. When will you be going?"

"I don't know yet. Daddy has to sort it out."

"Can I come with you?"

"I will ask my daddy," Emily said to Dottie. "Have you asked your mummy if you can have a puppy yet? Cause if you have a puppy you can come with me and Skye to agility classes."

Dottie said, "That would be good. I will ask my Mummy again."

When Dottie got home from school she said, "Mummy, Mummy," all excited, "can I have a puppy like Emily? Then we can both go to agility classes together."

"Hold on a minute," Dottie's mummy said. "I will have to speak to your daddy first."

"Oh, oh when will he be home?"

"Soon," she said. so Dottie went off to play with her toys.

While she was playing she could hear voices in the background. It was her mummy and daddy talking about what Dottie had asked for. Dottie's mummy called her down for her tea

While they were at the dinner table talking about everything that had gone on that day, Dottie's daddy said, "Your mummy says that you would like a puppy like Emily has got. Well we have had a long talk about it and we have decided that you can have one

on one condition, that it is your puppy and you have to train it and look after it."

Dottie jumped up and down in excitement saying, "Thank you, thank you. I will be able to go to agility training with Emily now."

Emily was playing in the school playground with all of the other children. In the background she heard Dottie calling, "EMILY, EMILY, my mummy and daddy said I can have a puppy."

"That's great!" They both danced around in excitement. "We can both go to training now."

Chapter 6

Dottie has her new puppy now. She asked Emily if she would like to come over to see it after school. Emily said that would be great, so she went round to Dottie's house to see her new puppy.

Emily said, "Awwww she is lovely. What are you going to call her?"

"I don't know. Would you like to help me pick a name?"

"Okay!" (Think, think, think!) All of a sudden Emily shouted, "I know, what about POPPY?!"

Dottie had a think. "Yes, yes, that is a lovely name for her. Yes I will call her Poppy."

Dottie called out to her mummy and daddy, "We have a name for the new puppy," she said, jumping up and down. Dottie was so excited, her mummy told her to calm down. Emily and Dottie were dancing around in excitement.

"Quiet, girls, what's her name?"

"POPPY, Poppy, Poppy."

"Oh that is a lovely name."

Both girls took their puppies down to puppy training for their first lesson. Their parents watched with amazement at how good they both were at making them sit and stay. Emily and Dottie had big smiles on their face's, both parents are so proud of their girls,

Both families went out for a picnic and they took the dogs with them. While they were all in the field having a good time, the girls started to practice what they had learnt at training classes like sit, stay and calling them back. Their parents were watching them and saying how good they were.

Emily said to Dottie, "Shall we make some jumps for Skye and Poppy?"

Yes lets."

The puppies were jumping over all of the jumps they had made. They were having such a good time.

The girls were amazed at the puppies, they were really good at it. "Let's try something else for them," said Dottie.

"What do you think?" said Emily.

But the girls couldn't think of anything, so they went over to their parents and asked them. Dottie's daddy said, "I know what, what about if we put some sticks out for them to run in and out of?"

Emily and Dottie shouted, "That sounds good." So off they all went to find the sticks and set them up.

They all had so much fun with the children and the dogs getting them to jump over the obstacles and running in and out of the sticks. Everyone was rolling around on the ground with the dogs and having a great time.

Chapter 7

It was now four months on and the puppies have got bigger, and they are growing into lovely dogs.

Emily and Dottie had just started agility classes as they had finished most of the main puppy training.

Both families went along to their first class. Emily and Dottie are very, very excited. Skye and Poppy were being very well behaved in the back of the car.

When they all arrived at the class there were lots of children and adults with their dogs, walking and running around the fields. They waited for the trainer to come over. Emily said, “It looks very scary!”

Dottie said, “Yes it does but I think it will be good fun.”

Emily’s and Dottie’s parents said, “You must go and say hello to everyone.” And off they went, to meet them.

The instructor said, “Hello everyone, I see we have two new dogs and owners today.” She went over to meet them. “What is your name?”

"I am Emily and this is Skye, say hello, Skye."
The instructor said hello to Skye. She put up her paw to say hello to the instructor. She moved onto Dottie. "And what is your name?"

"I am Dottie and this is Poppy, say hello, Poppy," and she put her paw up to shake hands.

The instructor called out to everyone to introduce Emily and Dottie and their dogs. At first they had to go round the course slowly to show the dogs what they had to do.

Now it was time to start the training. At first they had to entice the dogs over the obstacles and through the tunnels with food.

At first it was funny as the dogs ran all round the course and Emily and Dottie were showing them what to do, their parents could not stop laughing as it looked so funny.

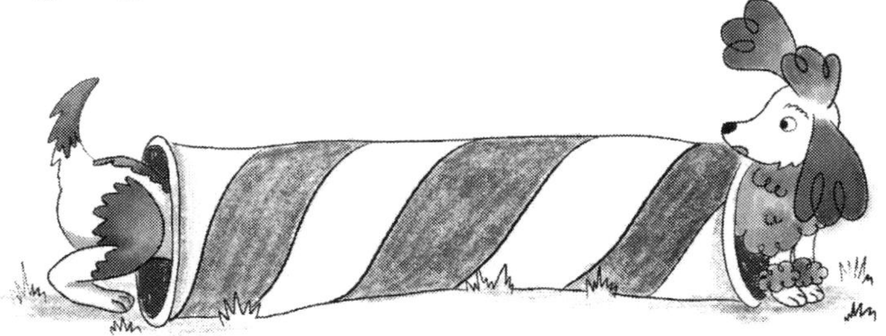

The girls were laughing so much the instructor had to ask them to take it seriously.

They both said, “Sorry, Miss, we will try harder this time.”

The girls started to take it more seriously and to the amazement of their parents and the instructor, they both showed that they had a natural talent. They could get both dogs to do what they wanted, through the tunnel, over the jumps, walking the plank and through the zigzag. When they had finished everyone gave them a big applause. Brilliant girls.

Chapter 8

Emily and Dottie have been going to agility class for some time now and they are very good at it. Their parents are so proud of them and they tell everyone how clever they both are.

It is now coming up to their first competition and they are both very nervous. The instructor and their parents said you will do well, both are so good. "Thanks, Mummy and Daddy," they said.

It was the day of the competition, and they were all very nervous. The girls waited in the background waiting for their turn, then all of a sudden Emily's name was called out,

"NOW we have Emily and Skye."

They both came out and everyone cheered and clapped as they entered the arena. Emily looked very nervous, then everyone went quiet so that she could start. Off she went through the tunnel, walking the plank, over the jumps and through the zigzags. Emily had a big smile on her face as she finished, they all clapped and cheered as she went out of the arena.

Now it was Dottie's turn,

"NOW we have Dottie and Poppy."

As she came into the arena everyone cheered and clapped.

Dottie was very nervous as well. Off she went over the jumps, over the plank, through the tunnel and through the zigzag's. Dottie had a big smile on her face as she finished, everyone cheered and clapped as she ran into the back.

Dottie met up with Emily, both girls were exhausted but very happy, smiling and laughing with their parents. The instructor came over to congratulate them. "You both did very well, girls, we are so pleased."

Emily and Dottie were watching all of the other's taking their turn, Emily turned to Dottie and said they are good.

Dottie said, "Yes they are. Do you think they are better than us?"

“Well they have been going to classes longer then we have.”

Dottie said, “Do you think we will win anything?”

“Don’t know.” They carried on watching.

It was coming to the end of the competition and both girls went over to their parents, shouting at the top of their voices, "DO YOU THINK WE WILL WIN?!"

Their parents said, "We will just have to wait for the judges to make their minds up." Both girls jumping in excitement.

"Will it be long?" they asked.

"We don't know, my darlings."

It was now time for the prizegiving. Both girls were very, very nervous, holding each other's hands very tightly,

The announcement came over the tannoy system.

"In third place we have Dottie and Poppy." Dottie was running around in excitement.

Her mummy said, "Go and get your prize." Off she went to collect it.

"In second place we have Kelly and Fred." Off they went to get their prize.

"And in first place we have Emily and Skye." She could not believe it. Off they both went to collect their prize. There were all cheering and clapping the winners.

Chapter 9

Emily and Dottie were jumping and running around in excitement, they couldn't believe they had won as it was their first competition. The smiles on their faces were wonderful to see.

Their parents went over to the girls to congratulate them. "You both are so clever, we're so proud of you," and gave them big hugs.

On their way home Dottie and Emily kept looking at their trophies. "Where can we put them, Mummy?" Emily asked.

Her mummy said, "In the cabinet for everyone to see."

Dottie asked her mummy where can we put her trophy. Her mummy said, "We can put it in the cabinet so everyone can see it."

It had been a very long day for the girls, they couldn't stay awake any longer. Emily's mummy looked in the back of the car to see both girls fast asleep cuddling their trophies.

The next day Emily and Dottie's parents got together to do a surprise party for them. It was very hard to keep it a secret as the girls were playing in the garden with the dogs but kept asking what they were doing.

Mummy replied, "It's a secret. You will find out soon."

"Oh OK," they both replied, and continued playing in the garden and singing, "It's a secret, it's a secret, it's a secret, hehehehehe."

Emily's and Dottie's mummies called them in. When they both got to the back door they were stopped. "Right girls, close your eyes," their mummies said as they guided them in. They then said, "Ready, open your eyes."

Their faces were a picture. "Oh, oh, oh, oh, Mummy, Daddy!" they shouted. "It's lovely."

Lots of food, big banner saying congratulation and special food for Skye and Poppy, they all had a lovely party.

On Monday both girls had to go to school. Emily said, “Mummy, can I take my trophy to school?”

“Yes,” she said. “But be careful with it,”

When she got to school Emily went straight to her teacher, Miss Jones, to show her the trophy. Miss Jones was very pleased for her, then Dottie came in and showed Miss Jones her trophy as well.

“Oh girls, you are both so clever. Shall we show the rest of the class?”

“Can we?” they asked.

Everyone all came into the class and sit down. Miss Jones said, “Quiet please we have some good news for you all. Emily and Dottie had their first dog agility competition at the weekend and they both won.”

Emily and Dottie went to the front of the class to show them their trophies. All of the class congratulated them and they all cheered and clapped. Emily and Dottie walked round the class to show them their trophies, they were all so happy for the girls.

Emily and Dottie had big smiles on their face's they were both so happy.

Then the class all shouted, "THREE CHEERS FOR EMILY AND DOTTIE. HIP, HIP, HOORAY, HIP, HIP, HOORAY, HIP, HIP, HOORAY

Emily and Dottie went on winning more competitions with their lovely dogs, Skye and Poppy.

About the Author

I am a mother of two and have seven grandchildren and one great-grandchild. I have not as yet seen my great-grandchild because of lockdown but looking forward to seeing him soon. I'm retired now and enjoying being at home and writing more stories for the children.